FISH

BY BRENDAN KEARNEY

One cold, dark morning, Finn and his dog, Skip, were woken early
by their alarm clock. The rest of the world was still fast asleep.

"Time to wake up!"

Finn yawned as he got dressed and packed up his things ready to go fishing. But Skip, with his eyes barely open, stretched and went back to sleep.

It was so early that the sky was still dark and
the moon and stars were shining brightly.

"Come on sleepy head! The fish won't catch themselves!" Finn whispered
quietly to Skip, as they crept through the empty streets toward the sea.

When they reached the shore, they found their small,
wooden boat hiding among the giant fishing boats.

Finn loaded their lunch and fishing rod into the boat,
pushed it out onto the water, and hopped aboard.

With the open ocean ahead of them, Finn rowed eagerly
while Skip watched the seals play in the wake of the little boat.

Skip thought some of the seals looked sad, but he didn't know why.

They pushed through the crashing waves to their favorite fishing spot.

Finn cast out his fishing line as far as he could...

and they waited and waited...

but not a single fish tugged at the line.
The ocean appeared to be empty as far as the eye could see.

Suddenly, Skip spotted something bobbing in the waves...

and with a huge SPLASH he jumped in to investigate.

After some time, Skip scrambled back into the boat, holding a ball he had rescued in his mouth. Litter flew everywhere as he shook himself dry.

"Ugh, Skip! Look at all that garbage! There are plastic bags
and bottles everywhere," Finn cried with disgust.

"Where are all the fish?" Finn wondered, as he scooped his net through the water. Every time he pulled it out, he was disappointed to find it filled with trash.

Before long, the small boat was almost sinking under the weight of all the things they had pulled from the ocean. "We haven't caught a single fish all day!" Finn sobbed.

The sun was beginning to sink in the sky, and their tummies were rumbling loudly. "We've got no choice but to row back, old friend," said Finn, patting Skip gently on the head, and starting to row slowly back to shore.

"Hello!" shouted a little girl, as Finn was pushing the boat up the beach. "Can we help you with that?"

"We're beach cleaners!" the girl explained. "We pick up litter that has been washed ashore by the tide, so that it doesn't get swept back into the ocean. We can help you with your pile of garbage—where did you find it all?"

"We scooped it out of the ocean while we were trying to catch a fish for dinner," Finn answered.

"But we didn't see a single fish all day!"

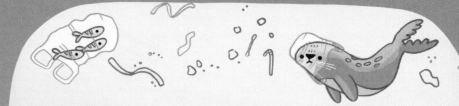

"That's no surprise! Trash, especially plastic, in the oceans across the world is harming wildlife. Sometimes animals get trapped in it, which can cause them to suffocate.

If animals eat the trash, it can poison them, or fill up their stomachs so they don't have room for real food."

"There is lots of plastic in the ocean and it doesn't get cleaned up.

Plastic litter, and even plastic that has been put in the garbage and taken to landfill sites, can easily be carried away by wind or rain. It often ends up in rivers or drains which can lead to the ocean."

"Once the plastic is in the ocean, it doesn't rot away—it stays there forever! It breaks down into smaller and smaller pieces of plastic, called microplastics. These poison wildlife and can even get into the water that humans drink, and our food, too!

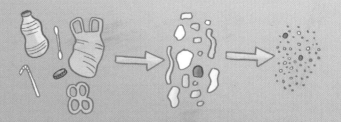

We need to reduce plastic in the oceans because they are home to a huge variety of wildlife.

Big changes start with small steps—there are lots of things we can do to help."

"We can throw away or recycle our waste correctly to make sure it doesn't litter the environment."

Paper

Glass

Cans

"We can repair and reuse our old things instead of buying more and throwing it away into a landfill.

We can use other things in a different way if they can't be repaired."

"We can avoid using single-use (non-recyclable) plastics such as plastic bags, drink cups, and water bottles.

Instead, we can choose to use things that can be recycled or that break down.'"

"We can tell our friends and family to get involved and start making small changes, too. It's fun!"

The following day Finn recycled everything he could.

He repaired everything
that could be fixed...

and he found other ways of
using what couldn't.

And he invited his friends and family
to help clean up litter on the beach.

Finn, Skip, and their friends continued to do what they could for the oceans, and clean the beach regularly. The more they did, the cleaner their surroundings became, and wildlife began to return to the sea.

Everyone felt so proud of what
they were doing to protect the oceans.

What will you do?

BRENDAN KEARNEY

Brendan Kearney lives and works by the sea in South West England with his little dog, Crumble. He has loved drawing since he started scribbling as a child and feels very lucky to be able to draw for a living. He particularly enjoys drawing animals (especially sea life!) and making up stories.

The idea for *Fish* was born from a fascination with the ocean and the animals that live in it. Living by the sea himself, Brendan is constantly reminded of the threats our oceans face, pollution being just one of them. He hopes that this book might help us to think twice about the amount of trash we throw away and what we can do to reduce our own waste.
He loves playing guitar and eating cookies, but absolutely hates slugs.

Penguin Random House

Produced for DK by Plum 5 Ltd

Editor Sophie Parkes
Designer Brandie Tully-Scott
Senior Editor Shannon Beatty
Jacket Coordinator Issy Walsh
Publishing Manager Francesca Young
Production Editor Marc Staples
Production Controller Basia Ossowska
Creative Director Helen Senior
Publishing Director Sarah Larter

First American Edition, 2020
Published in the United States by DK Publishing
1450 Broadway, Suite 801, New York, NY 10018

Published in Great Britain by Dorling Kindersley Limited
A catalog record for this book
is available from the Library of Congress.
ISBN 978-0-7440-2146-2

DK books are available at special discounts when purchased in bulk for sales promotions, premiums, fund-raising, or educational use. For details, contact: DK Publishing Special Markets, 1450 Broadway, Suite 801, New York, NY 10018
SpecialSales@dk.com

Printed and bound in China

For the curious
www.dk.com